Betsey's Birthday Surprise

EAST SUSSEX COUNTY COUNCIL

WITHDRAWN

D0263028

Also by Malorie Blackman

The NOUGHTS & CROSSES sequence:
NOUGHTS & CROSSES
KNIFE EDGE
CHECKMATE
DOUBLE CROSS

NOBLE CONFLICT

BOYS DON'T CRY

THE STUFF OF NIGHTMARES
TRUST ME
PIG-HEART BOY
HACKER
A.N.T.I.D.O.T.E.
THIEF!
DANGEROUS REALITY
THE DEADLY DARE MYSTERIES
DEAD GORGEOUS
UNHEARD VOICES
(A collection of short stories and poems, collected by Malorie Blackman)

For younger readers:
CLOUD BUSTING
OPERATION GADGETMAN!
WHIZZIWIG and WHIZZIWIG RETURNS
GIRL WONDER AND THE TERRIFIC TWINS
GIRL WONDER'S WINTER ADVENTURES
GIRL WONDER TO THE RESCUE

BETSEY BIGGALOW IS HERE!
BETSEY BIGGALOW THE DETECTIVE
MAGIC BETSEY
HURRICANE BETSEY

For beginner readers:
JACK SWEETTOOTH
SNOW DOG
SPACE RACE
THE MONSTER CRISP-GUZZLER

Betsey's Birthday Surprise

Malorie
Blackman

Illustrated by Jamie Smith

RED FOX

BETSEY'S BIRTHDAY SURPRISE
A RED FOX BOOK 978 1 782 95188 9

First published in Great Britain in 1996 by Piccadilly Press Ltd

This edition published by Red Fox,
an imprint of Random House Children's Publishers UK
A Random House Group Company

This Red Fox edition published 2014

1 3 5 7 9 10 8 6 4 2

Text copyright © Oneta Malorie Blackman, 1996
Illustrations copyright © Jamie Smith, 2014

The right of Malorie Blackman to be identified as the author of this work has been asserted
in accordance with the Copyright, Designs and Patents Act 1988.

All rights reserved. No part of this publication may be reproduced, stored in a retrieval
system, or transmitted in any form or by any means, electronic, mechanical, photocopying,
recording or otherwise, without the prior permission of the publishers.

The Random House Group Limited supports the Forest Stewardship Council® (FSC®),
the leading international forest-certification organisation. Our books carrying the FSC
label are printed on FSC®-certified paper. FSC is the only forest-certification scheme
supported by the leading environmental organisations, including Greenpeace. Our paper
procurement policy can be found at www.randomhouse.co.uk/environment.

MIX
Paper from
responsible sources
FSC® C016897
www.fsc.org

Set in Bembo MT

RANDOM HOUSE CHILDREN'S PUBLISHERS UK
61–63 Uxbridge Road, London W5 5SA

www.**randomhousechildrens**.co.uk
www.**totallyrandombooks**.co.uk
www.**randomhouse**.co.uk

Addresses for companies within The Random House Group Limited can be found at:
www.randomhouse.co.uk/offices.htm

THE RANDOM HOUSE GROUP Limited Reg. No. 954009

A CIP catalogue record for this book is available from the British Library.

Printed and bound in Great Britain by CPI Group (UK) Ltd, Croydon CR0 4YY

For Neil and Lizzy,
with love as always.

EAST SUSSEX SCHOOLS LIBRARY SERVICE	
567303	
Askews & Holts	Sep-2014
JF	£5.99

Malorie Blackman has written over sixty books and is acknowledged as one of today's most imaginative and convincing writers for young readers. She has been awarded numerous prizes for her work, including the Red House Children's Book Award and the Fantastic Fiction Award. Malorie has also been shortlisted for the Carnegie Medal. In 2005 she was honoured with the Eleanor Farjeon Award in recognition of her contribution to children's books, and in 2008 she received an OBE for her services to children's literature. She has been described by *The Times* as 'a national treasure'. Malorie Blackman is the Children's Laureate 2013–15.

Contents

The Best Guard Dog in the World!

"Oink! Oink! Oink! Oink!"

Betsey snuffled into the kitchen where the whole family were sitting down to breakfast. She snuffled along the ground and oinked again!

"Betsey child, what're you doing?" Gran'ma Liz frowned.

"I'm a pig!" Betsey announced.

"Tell us something we don't already know!" laughed Sherena, Betsey's bigger sister. "You eat like a pig and thanks to you, our room looks like a pigsty!"

"No, you don't understand. I'm going

to spend this weekend being all kinds of different animals," Betsey explained.

"Uh-oh!" said Desmond, Betsey's bigger brother.

"I don't like the sound of that," said Sherena.

"Sounds like another of Betsey's ideas," Mum sighed and poured herself another cup of coffee.

Gran'ma Liz just shook her head.

"I know I'm going to be sorry I asked this, but why d'you want to be all kinds of different animals?" asked Sherena.

"So I can see what it's like, of course," Betsey replied. "Then I can compare it to being a girl. Mrs Rhodes, my teacher, said that we have to think about which animal we'd most like to be and then say why in class. Well, I can't decide until I've tried to be some of them, can I?"

"Betsey, I'll say one thing for you –

you're different!" said Sherena.

"No, I'm not. I'm a pig!" said Betsey. "Oink! Oink!"

"Betsey, you're getting in everyone's way. Sit down and eat your breakfast," said Gran'ma Liz.

"Couldn't you put it on the floor for me?" asked Betsey. "Pigs don't eat at a table with a knife and fork."

"Elizabeth Ruby Biggalow, you will sit at the table and eat with this family or go without," said Gran'ma firmly.

Uh-oh! There it was again. Whenever Gran'ma Liz used Betsey's whole, full name, Betsey knew she'd better pay close attention! She stood up at once. Botheration! Being a pig didn't last very long – and she was just getting into it as well! Betsey sat at the table and had a long, hard think.

What animal can I be now? she wondered. Then she had a wonderful idea.

"Sherena, can I borrow your saucer?" Betsey asked.

Puzzled, Sherena lifted up her cup of coffee and handed over the saucer underneath it. Betsey poured some orange juice out of her glass and into the saucer.

"Betsey, what—" But before Sherena could say another word, Betsey bent her head and started lapping at the orange juice.

"Betsey, stop that! It's going all over the table," said Gran'ma Liz.

"Miaow!" said Betsey. And she carried on lapping at her orange juice.

"Elizabeth Ruby Biggalow . . ." said Gran'ma Liz ominously.

Betsey stopped lapping at once. Gran'ma Liz had used her whole, full name *twice* in less than five minutes!

"But Gran'ma, this is how cats drink," Betsey protested.

"Cats don't drink orange juice," Desmond pointed out. "They drink milk."

"Yeuk!" Betsey's face scrunched up at the thought of it.

"Find some other animal to be," Gran'ma Liz ordered. "As a pig you're in the way and as a cat you're too messy."

And with that Gran'ma Liz scooped up the saucer and placed it in the sink – so that was the end of that! Betsey sighed and straightened up. It wasn't easy being any kind of animal with Gran'ma Liz around!

"Betsey, no more animals at the breakfast table, if you don't mind," said Gran'ma Liz.

Betsey picked up her glass of orange juice and began to drink. Drinking as a cat was much more fun!

After breakfast, when all the dishes had been washed and dried and put away, Betsey had another think about what else she could be. She had to become an animal that wasn't in the way and wasn't messy . . .

"Got it!" Betsey said happily.

She went out into the living room and lay down on the floor. She put her hands at her sides and her feet together and started slithering and wriggling.

"Betsey, have you seen my glasses?" Gran'ma Liz walked into the living room.

"Gran'ma Liz, don't step on me," Betsey said quickly.

And only just in time too. One more step and Gran'ma Liz would've stepped on Betsey for sure.

Betsey carried on slithering and wriggling.

"What on earth are you doing, child?" Gran'ma Liz asked.

"I'm a worm," Betsey replied. "But I'm not making much progress. I've only moved a few centimetres. It must be hard work being a worm. And you almost stepped on me. So it must be quite dangerous being a worm too."

"It's harder work being your grand-mother," said Gran'ma Liz. "Betsey, get up off the floor. You'll ruin your clothes."

"But Gran'ma . . ."

"But nothing. Up. NOW!"

With a deep, deep sigh, Betsey stood up. Botheration plus one hundred!

"You're in the way as a pig, you're messy as a cat and you're underfoot as a worm!' said Gran'ma Liz. "I think that's enough animals for one day."

And that was that! Botheration plus one million!!

All day long, Betsey racked her brains.

What animal could she be that *wouldn't* upset Gran'ma? Maybe she could be a chirp-chirping bird? No. Gran'ma would say she was too noisy! Maybe she could be a flying fish – splish-splashing in the bath tub. No. Gran'ma Liz would say she was too wet!

Later that night, as Betsey put on her pyjamas to go to bed, she said to her dog, "Oh Prince! This is a lot harder than I thought it would be."

"Woof!" Prince agreed.

As Betsey climbed into bed, she still hadn't decided on which animal she could be.

"I'll think about it in my sleep," Betsey yawned. "Then I'm bound to get an answer."

And with that Betsey pulled the bed clothes up around her neck, closed her eyes and was asleep in less than a minute.

Betsey opened her eyes and was instantly awake. It was the middle of the night. Silvery moonlight streamed in through the window. Betsey sat up and took a

look around. Something had woken her up but Betsey wasn't sure what it was. Creak! Creeeee-eeeak! There it was again. Someone was creeping through the house . . .

"Sherena . . . Sherena . . ." Betsey hissed at her sister.

Creeee-eeeak! The strange noise sounded again. Betsey slipped her feet into her slippers and crept towards her sister's bed.

"Sherena . . ."

But Sherena wasn't there . . . Betsey knew what had happened at once.

"Prince! Prince!" Betsey whispered to

the dog lying beside her bed. "Wake up! There are kidnappers in the house. And they've got Sherena!"

But Prince refused to budge. He lay beside Betsey's bed, his head on his front paws and his eyes tight shut. Betsey's heart pounded like a sledge hammer as she tip-toed to the bedroom door. She was terrified. There were kidnappers in the house. Betsey had to get to Mum and Gran'ma Liz. But how could she do it? She looked back at Prince.

Huh! Some guard dog you are! Betsey thought with disgust.

Guard dog... That was it! Betsey thought of a way to wake up Mum and Gran'ma Liz without the kidnappers getting to her first. Betsey opened her bedroom door and got down on all fours so that the kidnappers wouldn't spot her.

"WOOF! WOOF!" Betsey barked at the

top of her voice. "ARFF! ARFF! WOOF!"

Then everything happened at once. There was a bang and a crash in the living room, followed by the lights being switched on in Mum's and Gran'ma Liz's bedrooms.

"WOOF! ARFF!" Betsey barked even louder. Her throat was getting sore but she wasn't going to stop now. At long last Prince joined in, but Betsey was louder.

"What on earth is going on?" Gran'ma Liz came out into the living room and switched on the light.

There lay Sherena, sprawled out on the floor. And next to her was a puddle of spilt orange juice, an empty plate and chocolate biscuits scattered here, there and everywhere.

"Sherena, what d'you think you're doing?" Mum frowned.

"I was hungry so I decided to have a snack." Sherena sat up. "But when Betsey started making all that noise, it startled me and I tripped over."

"You wanted a snack at three o'clock in the morning?" Mum said crossly. "Sherena, clean up that mess and go straight back to bed."

"Betsey, was it you making that racket?" asked Gran'ma Liz.

"I thought Sherena was being kidnapped," said Betsey. "And I wanted to wake up you and Mum without the kidnappers getting me! So I decided to be a guard dog!"

"Well, you woke us up, all right," said Gran'ma Liz. "I should think you've woken up the whole street as well!"

"I make an excellent guard dog," Betsey decided. "I know! That's what I'll be in class on Monday − the best guard dog in the world."

"Betsey, I prefer you as a girl," sniffed Sherena. "Then I wouldn't have got caught and I could've had my snack in peace!"

"Betsey, you can be a guard dog any time you like." Mum smiled. "I feel very safe knowing that you're in the house!"

Betsey's Birthday Surprise

The moment Betsey opened her eyes, she expected wonderful, sun-shiny, brilliant surprises. Well, she got a surprise all right! A nasty surprise. A *horrible* surprise. Everyone had forgotten her birthday!

At first Betsey couldn't believe it. Botheration! How could everyone have forgotten that today was her birthday?

"Gran'ma Liz, guess what today is?" Betsey asked hopefully.

"Saturday," said Gran'ma Liz. "Now run along and play, Betsey. I've got things to do."

Betsey decided to give Gran'ma Liz a teeny-tiny clue.

"Gran'ma, haven't you forgotten something?" Betsey asked. "Something wonderful about the day and *me*."

If Gran'ma Liz didn't get it from that then she didn't deserve to call herself a gran'ma!

"Betsey child, what are you talking about? It's Saturday. That's it! End of story! And . . ." Gran'ma Liz slapped her hand against her forehead. "I'd forget my head if it wasn't glued to my neck! Thanks for reminding me, Betsey. I promised

your mum I'd make some of her favourite biscuits for when she comes home from work. I'd better get started."

"But . . . but . . ." That's not what Betsey meant at all!

"Do you want to help me?" asked Gran'ma Liz.

No way! Not today of all days. It looked like Gran'ma Liz really *had* forgotten. Betsey wandered out into the back yard. Sherena bowled a cricket ball to Desmond who hit it into the dirt.

"Why the glum face, Betsey?" asked Sherena as she picked up the ball.

"Because today is . . . today is . . ."

"A kind of nothing day," Sherena said,

finishing Betsey's sentence. "I know exactly what you mean. There's nothing special going on. There's nothing to see, nothing to do. And it's the kind of day when you don't want to do anything either."

Betsey really couldn't believe it. All week she'd reminded everyone that it was her birthday on Saturday and they'd still forgotten. How *could* they? Even May hadn't sent a card. Betsey felt tears prick at her eyes.

"Sherena, I can't practise hitting the ball if you don't throw it to me," Desmond called out from the other end of the back yard.

"D'you want to stay and play cricket with us?" Sherena asked Betsey. "You can be the wicket keeper if you like."

"Stuff the wicket keeper!" Betsey snapped.

"Charming!" Sherena raised her eyebrows as Betsey flounced back into the house.

So it was true. They had all forgotten. Maybe Mum hadn't – but she wasn't here. But the rest had! There were no cards, no presents. As for a birthday cake? There wasn't even a birthday sandwich! Betsey would have settled for a birthday biscuit!

"Then I'll just have to do something on my own!" Betsey muttered.

Yeah! That's what she'd do. She'd celebrate her own birthday – all by herself. She'd show them all. She needed to do something fun to cheer herself up. Something *different*!

"I know!" Betsey clapped her hands.

She marched into Mum and Dad's bedroom. She switched on Mum's radio to listen to some dance music. That would cheer her up for a start. Then Betsey sat at the dressing-table and picked up Mum's most expensive bottle of perfume. Dad had bought it especially for her the last time he came home.

"I have to smell nice on my birthday," Betsey mumbled. She squirted some on her wrists . . . and her neck . . . and behind her ears . . . and on her feet and her legs . . . and her arms . . . and reached around to squirt some up and down her back. That was more like it! Hang on! Betsey began to cough. Mum's perfume sure was strong! Maybe she shouldn't have put on so much? Perhaps the smell would lessen in a minute or two.

What now? Betsey spotted the very thing. She opened Mum's jewellery box and put on a pair of Mum's long dangly earrings and her matching long, dangly necklace.

"I have to sparkle on my birthday!"

Betsey smiled at herself in the dressing table mirror.

"Clothes!" Betsey announced. "That's what I need!"

She definitely needed some birthday clothes. She opened Mum and Dad's wardrobe. She saw the very thing. Mum's favourite dress. It was midnight blue with sparkly, silvery sequins around the neck and the hem. Betsey pulled it off the hanger. She slipped off her own clothes and put on Mum's dress. It only reached to Mum's knees but on Betsey it trailed onto the floor. It didn't look too bad though. Betsey reached up on tip-toes to get Mum's hat – the one with a wide brim that she always wore to weddings. Betsey put it on and tilted it off at an angle, just the way Mum wore it.

"Perfect! Now I really do look like a birthday girl," Betsey said, admiring

herself in the mirror. "Wait until everyone sees me. I'd better turn off the radio. I don't want anyone to come in until I've finished. That would spoil the surprise. Now, what else can I do for my birthday?"

Betsey was just looking around the room, when she heard, "Betsey, could you come here for a second?" Gran'ma Liz was calling her.

"Coming," Betsey replied. She tried to walk but tripped over the bottom of the dress. Betsey lifted up the hem and tried again. That was better! She opened the bedroom door and stepped out into the living room.

"Gran'ma Liz, how do I loo . . . ?" Betsey's voice trailed off slowly.

"HAPPY BIRTHDAY, BETS—"

The living room was full to overflowing with Betsey's friends and their parents. May was there – and Josh and Celine and

Martin. Everyone was there. They'd all started to wish Betsey a happy birthday, but when they saw what she was wearing, their voices trailed off.

Betsey's voice had trailed off too. She stared and stared, wondering where all these people had suddenly come from.

"Elizabeth Ruby Biggalow, I . . . I . . ." For once Gran'ma Liz was lost for words!

One or two people started to titter. And three or four people started to giggle. Then the whole room erupted with laughter.

"Betsey, who told you to put on my best dress? And what on earth is that smell?" Mum choked. "Child, you smell like a perfume factory." And Mum marched Betsey into the bathroom.

"Why are all my friends here?" Betsey asked, amazed.

"Because I arranged a surprise party for you," said Mum.

"A surprise party!" Betsey's eyes gleamed. "For me?"

"You can rejoin it when you're wearing your own clothes and when you smell human again!" said Mum.

Whilst the bath was running, Mum stripped Betsey out of her dress. Betsey had to wash behind her ears and scrub her body until every trace of Mum's perfume had gone. Then when Betsey was wrapped in a warm, thick towel, Mum gave Betsey a box wrapped in glittery paper.

"Happy birthday, Betsey!" Mum smiled. "This is from your gran'ma and your dad and me."

Betsey tore off the paper in about two seconds flat. It was a dress. The most beautiful dress Betsey had ever seen. It was a sky-blue silk dress, covered with tiny, delicate flowers. Betsey put it on, then hugged Mum tight.

"Thanks, Mum," she said happily.

"Now isn't that better than my old dress which doesn't even fit you?" Mum smiled as she led the way into the living room.

As soon as everyone saw Betsey they all started clapping. They all agreed – Betsey looked wonderful.

"Well done, Betsey," said Uncle George, grinning. "We thought we'd surprise you with a party, but you had a surprise of your own!"

"It was my birthday surprise for all of you!" Betsey grinned.

"I'm only sorry I forgot my camera at home!" laughed May's mum.

"Thank goodness you did forget it," sniffed Gran'ma Liz. "Otherwise we'd never have lived it down!"

But only Betsey heard that bit!

Betsey Moves House

"Betsey, go and tidy your bedroom," Gran'ma Liz commanded.

"It's Sherena's turn," said Betsey.

"No, it isn't. I did it yesterday. It's your turn today," Sherena argued.

"But I wanted to play with May. We were going to play Robin Hood with my new bow and arrows," Betsey said. "Sherena, couldn't you do it for me . . . ?"

"Betsey . . ." Gran'ma Liz's voice held a warning.

"Oh, all right," said Betsey reluctantly. And off she went to tidy her room.

Ages later, when Betsey had finished, Gran'ma Liz said, "Betsey, it's your turn to help me tidy up the kitchen."

"It's Desmond's turn," Betsey protested.

"Oh no, it isn't. It's my turn tomorrow. It's your turn today," Desmond said.

"Oh, but . . ." Betsey began.

"Betsey!" There it was again – that warning note in Gran'ma's voice.

"It's not fair. It's just not fair," Betsey muttered under her breath. "If I had my own house, I could do what I liked when I liked and no one could boss my head."

"Did you say something, child?" asked Gran'ma Liz.

"No, Gran'ma," Betsey answered at once. And she followed Gran'ma into the kitchen to help with the tidying up.

When Betsey had finished, May came round. But by then Betsey was in a bad, bad mood.

"What's the matter with you?" May asked.

"I'm fed up! That's what's the matter," Betsey said. "I wish I had my own house and no one to tell me what to do!"

And that's when Betsey had her extra brilliant idea. It was such an exciting idea that Betsey couldn't help hopping up and down. Betsey took May by the hand and pulled her into the kitchen where Gran'ma Liz was reading her newspaper.

"Gran'ma Liz," Betsey began, "can I make a house in the back yard?"

"Pardon?!" Gran'ma Liz stared at Betsey.

"Can I make myself a house – a very small house – in the back yard?" Betsey repeated. "May will help me, won't you?"

"Sure! But how do we do it?" May asked.

Gran'ma Liz sat back in her chair. "I'd like to hear that too," she said.

"I'll make it with branches and leaves," Betsey announced. "I saw how it was done on the telly last week. I'll make myself a hut and then I can live there and have my own room and Sherena will have to tidy up our bedroom all by herself. Can I, Gran'ma? Please! *Please*!"

"Go on then." Gran'ma Liz smiled. "Just don't make a mess in *this* house."

Betsey skipped out to the back yard, followed by May. She was going to do it. She was going to make her very own house!

"Betsey, we can't make a hut. It'll be too difficult," said May.

"Not if we get some help!" Betsey smiled, and she pointed to her brother who was at the far end of the back yard with a drawing pad and a pencil in his hands. Betsey and May ran over to him.

"What're you doing?" asked Betsey.

"Drawing some chickens for a school project!" said Desmond. "I just wish they'd keep still."

"Desmond, I want to make a hut – right here in the middle of the back yard!" Betsey beamed. "Will you help me?"

"Why d'you want to do that?" Desmond asked. "And why should I help you?"

"Because I'll live in the hut instead of

the house and then none of you can tell me what to do," said Betsey.

"Well, if it'll get you out of the house, then I'll definitely help you," Desmond said at once. "We'll need long branches and banana leaves and palm fronds and loads of string."

"I'll get the leaves," said May.

"I'll get the string," said Betsey and she dashed into the house.

Ten minutes later, they all gathered in the back yard again. Desmond showed them how to set up the branches to make the frame of the hut and how to cover the branches with the leaves and fronds to make the walls. Then they each took long lengths of string and tied the leaves and fronds on to the branches.

It was very hard, hot work but at last it was all finished. They all stepped back to admire the hut.

"It looks wonderful," breathed Betsey. "Just like a real house."

"It's not bad at all," Desmond admitted.

"Desmond, you can't come in," said Betsey. "Not unless I say so, because it's my house."

"Thanks a lot!" sniffed Desmond. "Anyway, I've got homework to do, so you keep your house." And with that, off Desmond marched.

"That was a bit mean, Betsey," said May.

"Never mind him. Let's get some things to make my house more homely," said Betsey.

So off they went. Betsey gathered up her dolls, her bow and arrows and some of her books. Then she took the sheet and the pillow off her bed and into the back yard. In the meantime, May made some ham and tomato sandwiches.

"It's a bit cramped," said May, once everything was placed in the hut.

"That doesn't matter." Betsey smiled. "It's lovely and it's *mine*!"

They sat down to eat their sandwiches but the hut was so small they were squashed up against each other and their feet stuck out of the entrance.

"Shall we play a game?" May suggested after they'd finished eating.

"No, it'll make my new house untidy." Betsey shook her head.

"Your house is too small to get untidy," said May.

"You're the only one making my house untidy. And if you don't like my house you can always leave," said Betsey, crossly.

"I don't mind if I do." May crawled out of the hut and stood up. "I won't stay where I'm not wanted."

Betsey folded her arms as she sat in her house, getting crosser than cross. This was her house and she wasn't going to let May or Desmond in it, or anyone else for that matter. She was going to keep it all for herself. And that way it would stay clean and tidy and be all hers. Betsey looked around her house. It was small but perfect. She couldn't believe she had her very own home. The only trouble was . . . it was a bit lonely. There was no one to play with and no one to talk to.

"That doesn't matter," Betsey told herself.

But as she sat in her home, all alone, she began to feel that it did. What was the point of having her very own house if she didn't have anyone to share it with? The back yard was so quiet. She could hear the bamboo plants at the side of the yard, creaking as the wind blew through them, but that was all. She missed Gran'ma's laugh and Mum's voice. She missed Sherena's moaning and complaining. She missed May's company. She even missed Desmond teasing her. Betsey stuck her head out of the entrance to her hut. Grey clouds were scudding across the sky. Betsey crawled out of the hut and stood up in the back yard. She smiled up at the sky, then went into the main house. The whole family as well as May were sitting in the living room, watching telly.

"What are you doing here?" asked Desmond.

"I thought you had your own home now," said Gran'ma Liz.

"I do, but it's going to rain and my house isn't waterproof," said Betsey.

And sure enough, the moment she'd said that there came a flash of lightning and a clap of thunder. Giant raindrops hammered on the roof and the windows.

"See!" said Betsey, happily. "I told you it was going to rain."

"Quick, Betsey. Your house is going to be washed away," said Desmond, jumping up. "Come on. If we act now we can save it."

Betsey shook her head. "No, it's OK,

Desmond. That wasn't my real home. My real home is where my family and friends are."

"Betsey, that's a lovely thing to say." Gran'ma Liz smiled.

"And May, I'm sorry I was so mean about my house," said Betsey. "The next time I have a house, you can come in any time you want to."

"Are you going to make another one?" asked May.

"I might do," said Betsey. "But next time, I'll make it big enough for *everyone*!"

And just to show she meant it, Betsey gave everyone a hug – even Prince!

Betsey on the Telly

Betsey moved closer to the telly.

"Betsey child, you'll ruin your eyes if you sit that close to the TV screen," said Gran'ma Liz.

Betsey got up and stood in front of everyone.

"Betsey, move! I can't see," Sherena complained.

"I've decided I want to be on the telly," Betsey announced.

"Oh dear . . ."

"Another one of Betsey's ideas!"

Groans and sighs and shakes of the

head filled the living room!

"I'm serious. I want to be on there." Betsey pointed to the TV screen. "Gran'ma Liz, how do I get on the telly?"

"The only way you'll ever be on the telly is if you sit on it!" Desmond said before Gran'ma could reply.

"Desmond, behave!" said Gran'ma Liz, laughing.

"I mean it," said Betsey, crossly. "I want to be on the TV. Dad's coming home soon and it would be such a wonderful surprise for him."

"Your dad will be happy to see you in the flesh," said Gran'ma Liz. "He doesn't have to see you on the telly. Now come and sit next to me so we can all see the screen."

"But Gran'ma . . ."

"Betsey, I have no idea how you'd go about getting on the TV. You'll have to become an actress or go into politics or read the news or something like that," said Gran'ma Liz.

"Hhmm!" Betsey sat down next to Gran'ma but she wasn't watching the evening film any more. She was thinking hard. Betsey didn't know how yet but she *was* going to do it. One way or another she was going to be on the telly.

The next day was market day. But for once, Betsey wasn't even that excited about it. All the way there, Betsey was far too busy trying to work out how to get on the TV. At last they arrived at the market. It was full of hustle and bustle but Betsey hardly noticed any of it.

"Betsey, are you all right? You're very quiet," said Desmond

"Too quiet," Sherena agreed.

"I'm fine," Betsey said, still deep in thought.

Gran'ma Liz looked at Betsey very carefully but she didn't say a word. Instead she led the way to the fish stall first. Usually Betsey loved the smell of fish – salt fish, flying fish, crab, snapper . . . But not today. Betsey was still too busy trying to work out her problem.

46

And then she saw the answer! Over by the bread and cake stall was a thin man with a camcorder. The man moved his camcorder this way and that, filming the whole market. Betsey's eyes opened wider than wide. That man was filming! Maybe his film would be on the telly . . .

Betsey raced over to him and started jumping up and down in front of him.

"Betsey, what on earth are you doing? And don't run off like that," panted Gran'ma when she reached Betsey.

"I'm going to be on the TV," Betsey said proudly. And she carried on jumping up and down.

The thin man lowered his camcorder. "Er . . . I'm sorry, dear, but I'm just making a holiday video. I'm going to show all my friends back in England how wonderful this market is."

Betsey stopped jumping. "You're not making a programme for the telly?" she said, disappointed.

"I'm afraid not." The thin man shook his head. "Sorry!"

Gran'ma Liz led the way back to the others, warning Betsey not to run off again in case she got lost. As Betsey's family carried on walking through the market, Betsey felt a bit down.

"No!" Betsey muttered firmly. "I'm not going to give up. Not yet, at any rate."

And then she saw what she was looking for! A tall woman was holding a big microphone in her hand and talking to a stall holder in the market. Betsey grabbed hold of Gran'ma Liz's hand and rushed over to the tall woman.

"Hello! My name is Betsey Biggalow. Are you making a TV programme?" asked Betsey, hopefully.

The tall woman frowned down at Betsey. "No, I'm making a programme for the radio."

Betsey sighed. That wasn't the same thing at all!

"Betsey, come away. We've got shopping to buy," said Gran'ma Liz. "And please don't drag me all over the market."

The rest of the morning was spent buying groceries. Betsey looked up and down and back and forth, but no one looked like they were making a TV programme, so that when at last it was time to go home, Betsey wanted to cry. She was going to get on the telly or *burst*.

As they all walked up the road from the bus stop, Betsey lagged behind, trying and trying to think of a way of getting on the telly.

"Look! Dad's home already!" Desmond shouted.

With those words, Betsey forgot everything else and charged up the road. There was Dad, standing on the steps outside the front door. And he was holding something strange . . . Only when Betsey reached him did she realize what it was. Dad was holding a tablet device. Betsey was so surprised, her mouth fell open and she stared at Dad.

"Come on, Betsey. I'm filming you so do something!" Dad laughed.

"Where did you get that tablet from?" asked Desmond.

"I bought it," explained Dad. "And now I'm going to record the whole family. That way I'll have a video of all of you when I have to go away again. I can watch it every day to see all of you and hear your voices."

Betsey hopped up and down with joy. It wasn't going to happen *exactly* as she'd planned, she wasn't going to be on TV, but she was going to be filmed!

Dad filmed the whole family as they entered the house, all bubbling with laughter and chatting.

"Act normally!" said Dad.

And everyone did – except Betsey. She was too busy hogging the camera. It didn't matter which way Dad turned, Betsey was in front of him!

"Betsey, let other people get a look in!" said Sherena.

Dad spent the whole day filming – first Mum and Gran'ma Liz, then Sherena and Desmond, and finally it was Betsey's turn.

"What d'you want me to do, Dad?" Betsey asked.

"Anything you like," said Dad, pointing his tablet at Betsey. "You can sing or dance or say anything."

Betsey had a quick think. "I'll say something," she decided. "Dad, I'll be glad when you're a doctor and can come home for good – but I'm glad you're not one yet so you had to make this recording!"

Dad laughed.

"I wanted to give you something special that you can film and remember." Betsey walked over to Dad and gave him a great, big hug. "I love you, Dad, and this is one of my special hugs!"

"Every one of your hugs is special, sweet pea!" Dad smiled and he put down the tablet to hug her back. "OK everyone, it's time to see the results."

Everyone sat down on the sofa, eager

to see what Dad had come up with. Dad connected his tablet to the telly and started it up. The TV screen cleared and there was Mum sitting in the living room. And who was that creeping into the picture to sit at Mum's feet? Betsey! Mum smiled and

waved and said how much she missed Dad when he was away. Then it was Gran'ma Liz's turn.

Gran'ma Liz was in the kitchen singing.

She didn't realise Dad was filming her at first. When she did, she tried to shoo Dad away. But who was standing right beside her as she tried to stop Dad from filming her? Betsey! And who was that dancing behind Sherena and Desmond as they waved to the camera? Betsey. Betsey was everywhere!

"It's like watching the Betsey Biggalow show!" Sherena complained.

"Well, I did say I'd be on the telly," Betsey pointed out. "I just didn't realize how talented and brilliant I'd be!"

"You're a star, Betsey!" laughed Dad.

And no one could argue with that!